Frog on a log

Lesley Sims
Adapted from a story by Phil Roxbee Cox
Illustrated by Stephen Cartwright

Designed by Hope Reynolds and Helen Cooke
Edited by Jenny Tyler
Reading consultants: Alison Kelly and Anne Washtell

There is a little yellow duck to find on every page.

Frog lives beside a muddy bog.

Each day, he leaps up
from his log.

"I must keep fit!"
Frog starts to jog.

Frog jogs the whole way
round the bog.

One foggy day, Frog cannot jog.
Instead he sits down on his log.

But Pup
can't see Frog
in the fog...

And...

THUMP!

Pup bumps against the log.

Frog falls and SPLAT! He's in the bog.
"Oh dear," Pup barks.

Frog clambers back.
He's on his log.

Big Pig is lost
in all the fog.

And WHUMP!
Pig bumps against the log.

"Oh dear," grunts Pig.

The next day, sun shines on the bog.
Big Pig and Pup go back to Frog.

Frog grins. "Feel free to bump my log."

Big Pig and Pup think,
"Crazy Frog!"

"Just go ahead, Big Pig!" croaks Frog.
"This time I won't fall off my log."

Well, if you're sure...

They push the log.

Frog's right. He does stay on his log.

Frog AND the log fall in the bog!

Puzzles

Puzzle 1
Can you find the missing words?

Frog liked to ___.   log

Frog sat on a ___.   fog

Big Pig was lost in ___ .   jog

Puzzle 2
Choose the right speech bubble for the picture.

Puzzle 3
Spot the five differences between the two pictures.

Puzzle 4
Can you put these pictures in the order of the story?

A

B

C

D

E

Answers to puzzles

Puzzle 1

Frog liked to <u>jog</u>.

Frog sat on a <u>log</u>.

Big Pig was lost in <u>fog</u>.

Puzzle 2

Bump my log!

Puzzle 3

Puzzle 4

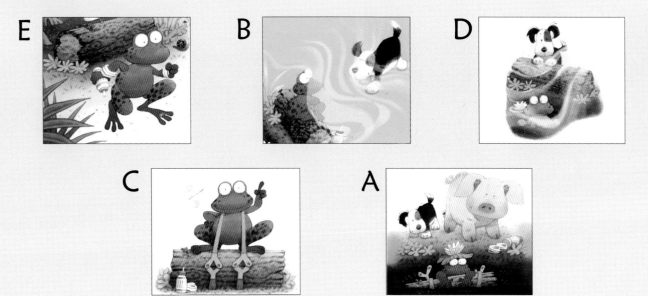

E

B

D

C

A

About phonics

Phonics is a method of teaching reading used extensively in today's schools. At its heart is an emphasis on identifying the *sounds* of letters, or combinations of letters, that are then put together to make words. These sounds are known as phonemes.

Starting to read

Learning to read is an important milestone for any child. The process can begin well before children start to learn letters and put them together to read words. The sooner children can discover books and enjoy stories and language, the better they will be prepared for reading themselves, first with the help of an adult and then independently.

You can find out more about phonics on the Usborne Very First Reading website, **Usborne.com/veryfirstreading** (US readers go to **veryfirstreading.com**). Click on the **Parents** tab at the top of the page, then scroll down and click on **About synthetic phonics**.

Phonemic awareness

An important early stage in pre-reading and early reading is developing phonemic awareness: that is, listening out for the sounds within words. Rhymes, rhyming stories and alliteration are excellent ways of encouraging phonemic awareness.

In this story, your child will soon identify the *o* sound, as in **frog** and **fog**. Look out, too, for rhymes such as **bump** – **thump** and **log** – **hog**.

Hearing your child read

If your child is reading a story to you, don't rush to correct mistakes, but be ready to prompt or guide if he or she is struggling. Above all, give plenty of praise and encouragement.